FAVORITE MOTHER GOOSE RHYMES

Old Mother Hubbard

Distributed by The Child's World®
1980 Lookout Drive • Mankato, MN 56003-1705
800-599-READ • www.childsworld.com

Acknowledgments
The Child's World®: Mary Berendes, Publishing Director
The Design Lab: Kathleen Petelinsek, Design and Page Production

Library of Congress Cataloging-in-Publication Data
Schwartz, Carol, 1954–
Old Mother Hubbard / by Carol Schwartz.
p. cm.
Summary: A retelling of the classic nursery rhyme, with end notes on the identity and origins of Mother Goose.
ISBN 978-1-60253-538-1 (library bound : alk. paper)
1. Nursery rhymes. 2. Children's poetry. [1. Nursery rhymes.] I. Mother Goose. II. Title.
PZ8.3.S389250l 2010
398.8—dc22 2010014154

Printed in the United States of America in Mankato, Minnesota.
July 2010
F11538

ILLUSTRATED BY CAROL SCHWARTZ

Old Mother Hubbard
went to the cupboard

to get her poor dog a bone.

But when she got there,

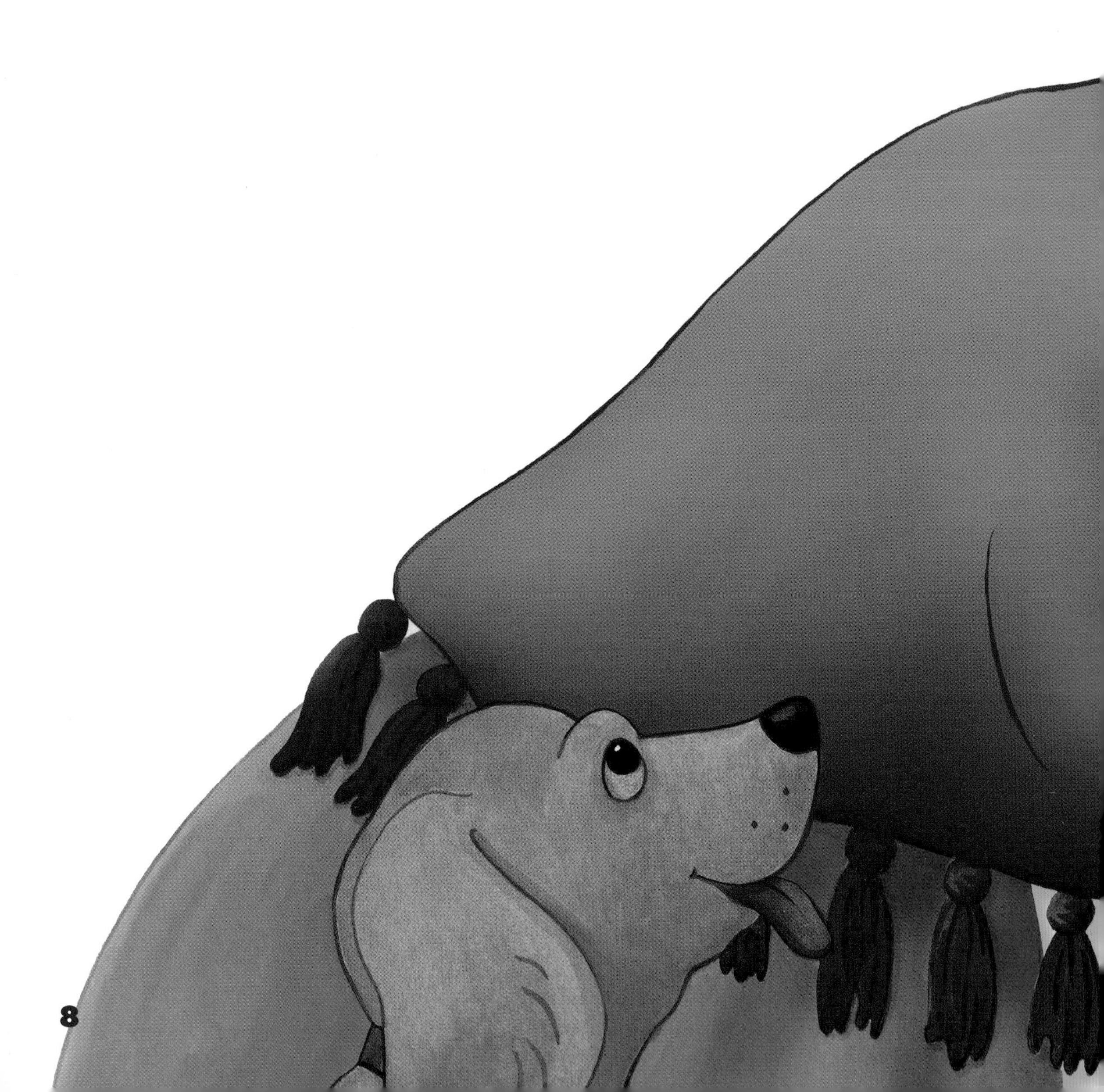

the cupboard was bare!

And so, her poor dog had none.

ABOUT MOTHER GOOSE

We all remember the Mother Goose nursery rhymes we learned as children. But who was Mother Goose, anyway? Did she even exist? The answer is . . . we don't know! Many different tales surround this famous name.

Some people think she might be based on Goose-footed Bertha, a kindly old woman in French legend who told stories to children. The inspiration for this legend might have been Queen Bertha of France, who died in 783 and whose son Charlemagne ruled much of Europe. Queen Bertha was called Big-footed Bertha or Queen Goosefoot because one foot was larger than the other.

The name "Mother Goose" first appeared in Charles Perrault's *Les Contes de ma Mère l'Oye* ("Tales of My Mother Goose"), published in France in 1697. This was a collection of fairy tales including "Cinderella" and "Sleeping Beauty"—but these were stories, not poems. The first published Mother Goose nursery rhymes appeared in England in 1781, as *Mother Goose's Melody; or Sonnets for the Cradle*. But some of the verses themselves are hundreds of years old, passed along by word of mouth.

Although we don't really know the origins of Mother Goose or her nursery rhymes, we *do* know that these timeless verses are beloved by children everywhere!

ABOUT THE ILLUSTRATOR

Carol Schwartz has been illustrating children's books for 21 years. She lives in Milwaukee, Wisconsin with her husband, dog, and cat. Carol's love of nature is inspired by the forest (and parade of wild creatures) that she sees from her studio windows.